Fit to Kill

by

Victor L. Cahn

SAMUEL FRENCH

FOUNDED 1830

NEW YORK HOLLYWOOD LONDON TORONTO

SAMUELFRENCH.COM

ISBN 978-0-573-66397-0   Printed in U.S.A.   #8223

IMPORTANT BILLING AND CREDIT REQUIREMENTS

All producers of *FIT TO KILL must* give credit to the Author of the Play in all programs distributed in connection with performances of the Play, and in all instances in which the title of the Play appears for the purposes of advertising, publicizing or otherwise exploiting the Play and/ or a production. The name of the Author *must* appear on a separate line on which no other name appears, immediately following the title and *must* appear in size of type not less than fifty percent of the size of the title type.

FIT TO KILL opened April 9, 2005 at the Clurman Theatre @ Theatre Row, 410 West 42nd Street in New York City, with the following cast:

ADRIAN BONHAM .... Patrick Melville

AMY COURTLAND .... Lanie MacEwan

JANICE BLAKE .... Jana Robbins

The producer was Rachel Reiner Productions. The director was Eric Parness. The scenic designer was Robert R. Sweetnam. The lighting designer was Pamela Kupper. The costume designer was Sidney Shannon. The sound designer was Nick Moore. The stage manager was Susan D. Lange.

FIT TO KILL premiered January 10, 2003 at Curtain Call Theatre in Latham, NY with the following cast:

ADRIAN BONHAM .... Howard Schaffer

AMY COURTLAND .... Agnes Elizabeth Kapusta

JANICE BLAKE .... Eva Dolan

The producer was Carol Max. The director was Steve Fletcher. The set designer was Jeffrey Guidice. The lighting designer was John E. Miller. The costume designer was Jeremy Buechner. The sound designer was Jeanne L. Stephenson. The stage manager was Gary Stromberg.

CHARACTERS

ADRIAN BONHAM, 38
AMY COURTLAND, 30
JANICE BLAKE, 45

SCENES

ACT I:
Scene 1: A chess club. Evening.
Scene 2: The house. The next evening.
Scene 3: The next afternoon.
Scene 4: Two days later.

ACT II:
Scene 1: The next evening.
Scene 2: The next evening.
Scene 3: Moments later.

SETTING

The primary setting is the living room of Janice and Adrian's house in Connecticut. The time is summer.

The room is elegantly furnished, and decorated with books and various pieces of fine art. At CENTER is a couch with matching chairs. At RIGHT is a bar, at LEFT a desk and chair. UPSTAGE is a chess table with pieces set up. OFF LEFT is a corridor that leads to the rest of the house. OFF RIGHT is the door that leads both outside and to the basement.

ACT I

Scene 1

(A chess club.)

(Summer. Evening.)

*(The lights come up on a single chair. **ADRIAN**, dressed elegantly, sits in contemplation.)*

ADRIAN. Knight to Bishop 4.

(pause)

VOICE. *(offstage)* Board Number 10: Knight to Knight 2.

(pause)

ADRIAN. Pawn To Rook 5.

(pause)

VOICE. *(offstage)* Board Number 11: Rook takes pawn.

*(From out of the darkness walks **AMY**. She wears a short skirt, a blouse, and high heels. She looks at him. For a moment, **ADRIAN** does not see her.)*

ADRIAN. Bishop to Knight Five.

(pause)

VOICE. *(offstage)* Board Number 12: Pawn to Knight 3.

*(**ADRIAN** turns, sees her, and stares with pleasure.)*

VOICE *(offstage)* Board Number 12: Pawn to Knight 3!

*(**ADRIAN** smiles at **AMY**. She smiles back.)*

VOICE *(offstage)* Board Number 12 –

ADRIAN. I heard you!

(short pause)

ADRIAN. *(continued)* Now listen carefully. Announce to Board Number 12 checkmate in six moves as follows: Rook to King 7; King Rook to Queen Bishop 1. Rook takes Knight Pawn, check; King to Bishop 1. Rook to Bishop 7, check; King to King 1. Rook to King 1, check; Bishop to King 3. Rook takes Bishop, check; King to Queen 1. Bishop to Bishop 6, checkmate.

> *(He grins at **AMY**, who grins back. Pause.)*

VOICE. *(offstage)* Board Number 12 resigns.

ADRIAN. Please congratulate Board Number 12 for a game well played.

> *(**ADRIAN** continues to scrutinize her.)*

VOICE. *(offstage)* Board Number 12 accepts and offers you the same.

ADRIAN. Thank you. Let us proceed.

VOICE. *(offstage)* Board Number 13: Queen takes Pawn.

ADRIAN. *(preoccupied with **AMY**)* Rook...rook to knight... seven.

> *(He smiles, then suddenly grimaces.)*

Wait a second! Let me change that to...uhhh...

VOICE. *(offstage)* I'm sorry, sir. The move has been transmitted. You'll have to play it.

> *(**ADRIAN** reacts with disgust. As he watches in fury, **AMY** smiles, then leaves.)*

ADRIAN. All right! Fine! Let's get on with it! Next board!

> *(a beat)*

C'mon! Next board!

> *(pause)*

VOICE. *(offstage)* Board Number 14...

> *(The lights dim quickly.)*

End of Scene 1

Scene 2

(The living room of Janice and Adrian's country house.)

(The next evening.)

(We hear the Andante from Mendelssohn's Piano Trio in D minor. As the lights come up, ADRIAN strolls in, adjusting another elegant outfit. He goes to the bar, carefully chooses a bottle, and pours himself a drink. He sniffs the contents, savors the bouquet, sips, then smiles. He ambles to the couch, where he luxuriates.)

(JANICE enters from outside, carrying a suitcase and an attaché case, with a handbag dangling by a long strap over her shoulder. She wears a business suit and pumps. She gazes at ADRIAN with amusement, then drops her suitcase, places her attaché case and handbag to the side, and presses a button on the sound system. The music stops.)

(ADRIAN frowns, then turns around and sees JANICE. At once, his face breaks into a smile. He sets down his drink and walks to her.)

ADRIAN. Sweetheart! I didn't expect you so soon!

JANICE. Caught an early flight. Hope I didn't interrupt anything.

ADRIAN. Not at all! Just contemplating the universe.

(They kiss warmly.)

I missed that.

JANICE. So did I.

ADRIAN. How'd everything go?

JANICE. Even better than I expected.

ADRIAN. Terrific! But you must be exhausted.

JANICE. Is that how I look?

ADRIAN. To the contrary, you look exhilarated.

JANICE. Good. Because that is exactly how I feel.

(She walks to the couch.)

ADRIAN. I can't wait to hear the report.

JANICE. In a minute, sweetheart.

    (She sits and kicks off her shoes.)

ADRIAN. Can you use a drink?

JANICE. In a minute.

    (She unbuttons her jacket.)

ADRIAN. Let me help.

    *(**ADRIAN** helps her remove the jacket, then puts it aside.)*

JANICE. Bring my case, will you?

ADRIAN. My pleasure.

    (He retrieves the case. She unbuttons the top of her blouse.)

    How was the flight?

JANICE. Stinkeroo.

ADRIAN. I'm sorry.

JANICE. Children should not be allowed in first class. Unless they're stored under the seats like luggage.

ADRIAN. Amazing how one kid can ruin a whole trip –

JANICE. This time there were three. Screaming, running up the aisles…

ADRIAN. Maybe they should be put in cages. Like pets.

JANICE. Let's not be cruel.

    (a beat)

    Only if they're under ten.

    (She opens her attaché case and removes papers that she peruses.)

ADRIAN. I took a few calls from the California office. They didn't leave names.

JANICE. Mind taking my bag upstairs? And where's my mail?

ADRIAN. Just where you like it.

    (He picks up the suitcase, then leaves up the stairs. She

goes to her desk, sits, and examines her mail, tearing and tossing most envelopes into a wastepaper basket.)

*(***ADRIAN*** *returns.)*

ADRIAN. *(continued)* All done.

(He walks to **JANICE** *and places his hands on her shoulders. She continues to go through her mail.)*

How we doin'?

JANICE. Feel like I've won a 10K race.

ADRIAN. Then you relax, and let me take over.

(He massages her shoulders.)

I didn't unpack. Did you want me to?

JANICE. I'll do it later. Besides, I have to put in clean things. I'm flying to Chicago tomorrow.

ADRIAN. Leaving so soon?

JANICE. Money to be made.

ADRIAN. But we haven't had any time together.

JANICE. Can't be helped.

ADRIAN. I'm not complaining.

JANICE. And I appreciate that.

ADRIAN. It's just that I like to keep up. In case you need me.

(She pats his hand on her shoulder.)

JANICE. Honey, *this* is what I need from you.

(Short pause. He continues massaging.)

ADRIAN. Oh! Ellen called this morning. She needed some figures from last year.

JANICE. I'll call her back.

ADRIAN. No rush. I took care of it.

JANICE. All by yourself? I'm impressed.

ADRIAN. No problem. Although I did want to ask one thing. If this isn't a bad time.

JANICE. 'Course not.

(She walks to the couch, where she stretches out and studies more papers.)

ADRIAN. I may be wrong, but I noticed that a lot of funds seem to move from one page to another. Even one book to another.

JANICE. You noticed that just this morning?

ADRIAN. The same totals also jump between different clubs.

JANICE. And your point is…?

ADRIAN. You're not doing anything illegal, are you?

JANICE. Adrian, I have no intention of losing anything because of crooked bookkeeping. The business is in perfect order.

ADRIAN. I should've known.

(He sits and massages her feet.)

Why didn't you fly directly to Chicago?

JANICE. I would've missed seeing you.

ADRIAN. That certainly makes me feel warm and fuzzy.

JANICE. And I wanted to touch base at the club here. Make sure nothing or no one is out of whack.

(a beat)

You can stop now.

ADRIAN. I thought it felt good.

JANICE. You're overdoing it.

(She kicks free. ADRIAN walks to the bar.)

ADRIAN. When I was in the city, I found a remarkable port we've been looking for.

(JANICE looks up.)

I've been looking for. Cockburn's, 1935.

(He holds out the bottle.)

And I was waiting for you before I opened it.

JANICE. I'll have my regular.

(He shrugs, puts down the bottle, opens another, and pours.)

ADRIAN. Well?

JANICE. What?

ADRIAN. Miami. What happened?

(He brings her the drink, then takes his own and sits near her.)

JANICE. Relax. You're still the richest chessplayer in the country. The firm now owns three new companies, purchased at rockbottom prices. Two will shortly go bankrupt, providing a useful write-off.

ADRIAN. How'd the owners take it?

JANICE. Former owners.

(She sips her drink, then puts it aside.)

They didn't like being bought out, especially by a woman.

ADRIAN. How could you tell?

JANICE. I recognized the look. They know they're talking to a former model, so they figure I'm either dumb or a front for the real boss.

ADRIAN. No matter how much a woman accomplishes, some men still think of her as a slab of meat.

(a beat)

JANICE. No one thinks of me as meat.

ADRIAN. You know what I mean.

JANICE. When I walked in, they started the usual way: looking up and down, snickering. Jenkins tried to be chivalrous: "Mizzzz Blake, why don't you sit at the head of the table?" As if, won't it be fun to pretend I'm a real executive? So I said, "Mr. Jenkins, wherever I sit *is* the head of the table."

ADRIAN. That line always works, doesn't it?

JANICE. One hour later, Mr. Jenkins' bloated belly was hanging over his belt, and he was puffing very hard. He was also missing a company.

ADRIAN. That's my little tycoon.

JANICE. Little?

ADRIAN. I was speaking of size, not stature. I had an interesting time last night. Played fifteen games. One was a curiosity. I opened Queen's Pawn, and the guy turned it into a Benoni Counter. Maybe he figured the novelty would throw me. Anyway, about the twentieth move, I was ready to fork him with my knight –

JANICE. One other thing.

(*a beat*)

I'm sorry! Weren't you finished?

ADRIAN. Not quite.

JANICE. You forked him with your knight. The end. Right?

ADRIAN. There was a bit more to it.

JANICE. Okay.

ADRIAN. It'll hold.

JANICE. You're sure?

ADRIAN. Go on.

JANICE. Nothing vital.

(*She goes to refill her drink.*)

I sold the Palm Beach apartment.

ADRIAN. Why?

JANICE. Why not?

ADRIAN. It's beautiful!

JANICE. It's too small, and I've never liked the view.

ADRIAN. It looks right out on the waterway!

JANICE. From the third floor. I don't like the third floor.

ADRIAN. It's not that bad –

JANICE. It's also a waste of money.

ADRIAN. We go to Florida at least twice a year!

JANICE. We can still go whenever we want. We'll just stay in a hotel.

ADRIAN. But I put a lot of thought into that place! The whole Southern island motif!

JANICE. Don't whine, darling.

ADRIAN. I'm talking about something I worked on for a long time –

JANICE. And that's why I got a great deal on it.

ADRIAN. I don't care about the deal! I like the apartment!

JANICE. The decision is made.

ADRIAN. Did you sign anything?

JANICE. I told you –

ADRIAN. Maybe we can get it back!

JANICE. The point is, I want to get rid of it.

ADRIAN. The point is, I like it!

JANICE. I don't.

ADRIAN. But I do!

JANICE. But I pay for it!

> *(a beat)*

> Darling, I don't want to pull rank. But I earn the money, so I decide how we spend it. When you help earn it, you can help decide.

ADRIAN. Sweetheart, we agreed to keep everything 50-50. What's mine is yours. And vice versa.

JANICE. Darling, everything I have is yours. But let's be fair. You don't kick in your fifty. So when a financial decision has to be made, I'm the one who makes it.

ADRIAN. Honey, I admit I don't bring in as much as you –

JANICE. Adrian, you don't bring in diddly.

> *(short pause)*

ADRIAN. My talent doesn't generate a great deal of income. But I'm not jealous.

JANICE. That's very mature.

ADRIAN. I think it's great that you've turned some simple skills like jumping and stretching into a…

JANICE. A multi-million-dollar conglomerate.

ADRIAN. I'm happy for you.

JANICE. You're also happy to live here like the Sheik of Abbi Babbi.

ADRIAN. I try to be supportive.

JANICE. Sweetheart –

ADRIAN. I don't know what you expect –

JANICE. Adrian!

ADRIAN. WHAT!?

   (short pause)

JANICE. What's with this tone of voice?

ADRIAN. I'm sorry.

JANICE. And I don't like that word.

ADRIAN. Which one?

JANICE. "Supportive." I don't care for it at all. Whenever a man uses it, he sounds as if he thinks the woman needs a hand, or that she plays at her job while he does the real work.

ADRIAN. I don't think of it that way.

JANICE. I do. After all, darling, you don't support me. I support you.

ADRIAN. I was using it in the metaphoric sense.

JANICE. However you're using it, lose it.

   (short pause)

ADRIAN. I had no idea I was such a burden.

JANICE. Don't pout.

ADRIAN. Am I in the way around here? Or just a tax deduction?

JANICE. A very sexy tax deduction.

ADRIAN. I'm serious!

JANICE. So am I. I enjoy showing you off.

ADRIAN. Sometimes you make me feel like a finely groomed poodle.

JANICE. I also enjoy a man who's secure enough to share my success.

ADRIAN. A lot of men couldn't handle it.

JANICE. A lot of men wouldn't want to.

   (short pause)

ADRIAN. What's that supposed to mean?

JANICE. Only that most husbands would be uncomfortable knowing their wife made a few thousand times more than they did.

ADRIAN. I have the strength of character to accept that knowledge gracefully.

JANICE. *(stroking him)* I also enjoy you another place. Your creativity in the bedroom remains much appreciated.

ADRIAN. Always a thrill doing it with such an eminent partner. A body worshipped by millions.

(They kiss passionately. JANICE breaks away.)

JANICE. That's what makes all this so painful.

ADRIAN. All what?

JANICE. On the plane today, I was thinking back. I used to love walking in with you to a dinner or cocktail party. You'd end up doing a memory demonstration or some other stunt that'd leave everyone speechless. I got a real kick out of it.

ADRIAN. Is this going somewhere?

JANICE. I also had fun watching my friends lust over a brilliant, adorable young husband who couldn't wait to do anything I asked.

ADRIAN. And they didn't know half of what I did.

JANICE. I was glad to pay for you because I knew I was nourishing an artist the world failed to appreciate.

ADRIAN. We live in vulgar times. Art like mine goes begging, while meretricious claptrap like…

JANICE. My videos?

ADRIAN. How can you even think that?

JANICE. I know you're frustrated.

ADRIAN. Never with you!

JANICE. But darling, you have to understand. Power changes people. And in my circles standards are strict.

ADRIAN. Are you implying I don't meet them?

JANICE. You still fool with games.

ADRIAN. I play chess! That's what I do!

JANICE. But *your* playing doesn't count. You see, when my crowd plays…well, let's say that we play to kill. In the metaphoric sense.

ADRIAN. That's ruthless even for you, isn't it?

JANICE. You're the one who dumped his first wife.

ADRIAN. She was nothing compared to you.

JANICE. I'm aware of that.

ADRIAN. You were someone – I mean, you *are* someone unique. Bright, eternally youthful –

JANICE. Wealthy.

ADRIAN. That has nothing to do with it.

JANICE. Even so, love, I'm worried about you.

ADRIAN. Why?

JANICE. It seems to me, and I hope I'm wrong, but I don't think I am, that you've cut down on your work. You've stopped writing and teaching. Instead you hang around here drinking wine, or you go to the city and throw away my money.

ADRIAN. Your money.

JANICE. The money I earn.

ADRIAN. All I do is make classic purchases that enrich our life.

JANICE. Adrian, we do not need that automobile showcase in our garage. We do not need to restock our cellar with the overflow from every vineyard in France. And *our* life is not enriched when you dress like the Duke of Windsor to buy monogrammed toilet paper.

ADRIAN. There's something to be said for maintaining quality in all aspects.

JANICE. Speaking of toilet paper…Adrian, you're slipping.

ADRIAN. How can you say that?

JANICE. You go to the weakest clubs, and take on mediocre players.

ADRIAN. Wait a minute –

JANICE. Everyone looks at you as if…well, I hate to say it…

ADRIAN. But you will!

JANICE. As if you're a freeloader. Or worse.

ADRIAN. I give exhibitions and lectures! I study games from all over the world!

JANICE. Darling –

ADRIAN. And I never stop promoting you! Boasting about your triumphs, as you lead your sisters to the glories of economic power!

JANICE. Don't be sarcastic.

ADRIAN. How many men would be so supportive?

JANICE. Careful.

ADRIAN. Sorry. Encouraging.

JANICE. Not much better.

ADRIAN. How about loyal? Faithful? Obedient?

JANICE. Work on it.

ADRIAN. I don't even mind when you tell everyone how badly you beat me at tennis.

JANICE. And golf. And racquetball. And –

ADRIAN. Most men would be intimidated. I'm proud!

JANICE. You're very sweet. But don't forget what I said.

ADRIAN. I'll give it my best.

JANICE. I'm so glad. Oh, one more thing. Your smile, your way with words, your boyish charm?

ADRIAN. Don't worry. I won't lose 'em.

JANICE. Seems to me they're sharper than ever. As if you've had too much practice.

ADRIAN. You think I'm seeing someone?

(She looks at him.)

C'mon! I admit I meet women. Everyone in the public eye does.

(She continues to look at him.)

We may have dinner. A couple have even visited this house. But sweetheart, to think I'd go any further, that's absurd! And let's face it. You meet plenty of people.

JANICE. We're talking about you.

ADRIAN. I know!

JANICE. And I've heard rumors.

ADRIAN. No!

JANICE. Yes.

ADRIAN. From whom? Tell me!

JANICE. A secretary here. A reporter there.

ADRIAN. And you believe them?

JANICE. You're a very attractive man.

ADRIAN. Janice…sweetheart…

JANICE. I know you have to fight them off.

ADRIAN. I'm flattered –

JANICE. But you're not fighting hard enough.

   (short pause)

ADRIAN. There's only one reason anyone would tell you these things.

JANICE. Because they're true?

ADRIAN. I'll bet some of your competitors are behind it. The men who can't stand to see a woman like you get ahead.

JANICE. What do you mean, "a woman like me"?

ADRIAN. A woman who's sexy *and* smart. A lot of men can't take it.

JANICE. Maybe. But sweetheart, let me tell you something. I've made a fortune helping women feel good about their bodies. Sometimes I think of all the clerks and housewives who have gone to my clubs and bought my videos. They're the ones who have paid for this house. And your cars. And your wine. And your clothes. The skinnies and the tubbies, the ones with the flat chests and the ones with the wide hips and the big butts. Every desperate one who hopes that if she buys the right leotard and sweats to the music, her grubby little life will be salvaged. They idolize me. They'd do anything I say. But most of them are so insecure, so…stupid, that the only time they feel good is when a man tells them that *he* feels good. And to get that approval, those women will do anything.

(a beat)

Fight 'em off, darling. Just as hard as you can.

(She heads for the corridor. He watches. She stops, turns, and points to her shoes. ADRIAN looks at her, uncertain. She snaps her fingers and points to her shoes.)

(He looks at the shoes, smiles, picks them up, and brings them to her.)

ADRIAN. Anything else I can do?

JANICE. Have you made dinner?

ADRIAN. You told me you were coming later.

JANICE. Then fix something now.

ADRIAN. You see, this is why we should have a maid. She could whip up a meal in no time!

JANICE. I don't want a maid. You can't imagine how much pleasure I get when my husband is in the kitchen, putting his love into my supper.

ADRIAN. Happy to help wherever I can.

(She smiles and leaves. He grimaces, and his hand tightens around the bottle of Cockburn's.)

End of Scene 2

Scene 3

(The next afternoon.)

*(**AMY**, again wearing a short skirt, a blouse, and high heels, studies a vase. **ADRIAN**, dressed with his customary elegance, appears and studies her.)*

ADRIAN. Hirado. A rare Japanese porcelain. Seventeenth century.

AMY. It's pretty. Odd shape, though.

ADRIAN. I like pretty things in all shapes.

AMY. And you don't mind mixing styles.

ADRIAN. If something appeals to me, I make it fit. For instance, that rug is Tibetan. And the oil is by Antonio Milone. The bedroom, on the other hand, is neo-classical.

AMY. I'd like to see it.

ADRIAN. I won't let you leave without a visit. From what I can see, you're another with an eye for quality.

(He fingers her blouse.)

Delicate material.

(She walks to a table.)

AMY. But I also appreciate something sturdy.

ADRIAN. English mahogany.

(She sits.)

Make yourself comfortable.

AMY. Thanks. I'm good at that.

ADRIAN. Something to drink? We have a generous assortment.

AMY. I'll leave it to you.

ADRIAN. Smart choice.

*(**ADRIAN** goes to the bar and pours two drinks.)*

AMY. You must love having such a big pool.

ADRIAN. Care for a dip?

AMY. I didn't bring a suit.

ADRIAN. Now we have two places to visit.

(He brings the drinks, gives one to her, and takes one for himself.)

This should meet with your approval.

(She sips.)

AMY. It's good. What year?

ADRIAN. Sherry has no year. Its glory is its simplicity.

AMY. Tasty.

ADRIAN. That's all? Tasty?

AMY. Very tasty.

ADRIAN. This is Williams and Humbert. The best.

AMY. Extremely tasty.

ADRIAN. Very old British firm. The only sherry, really.

AMY. Ever go for anything stronger?

ADRIAN. Intoxication is the recourse of a mind disappointed with itself. I find my own perpetually fascinating.

AMY. I can understand why. That was some chess thing the other night. I'd never seen one before.

ADRIAN. A blindfold simultaneous. "Simultaneous" means playing a group of opponents at once. "Blindfold" means without the board.

AMY. You always play fifteen?

ADRIAN. I've done as many as twenty. But that's blindfolded. With the board, 135.

AMY. That's incredible.

ADRIAN. Yes, it is.

AMY. You usually win them all?

ADRIAN. Usually.

AMY. What happened the other night?

ADRIAN. I lost one.

AMY. I know. How come?

ADRIAN. Sometimes they slip in a ringer. The rest are local fish who pay $25 a head for the privilege of losing.

AMY. What do you call them? "Fish?"

ADRIAN. Average players. Woodpushers. Fish. That was an exceptionally weak school. Except for…

AMY. One shark. $25 a head. How much do you keep?

ADRIAN. Is this the beginning of the interview?

AMY. It's been going on the whole time.

ADRIAN. No notebook? No recorder?

AMY. They make my subjects nervous.

ADRIAN. You ever forget details?

AMY. I never forget anything.

ADRIAN. You're a tribute to your profession.

AMY. A matter of experience. Learning to handle everyone's special needs. You were saying how much you make.

ADRIAN. About $1000 a performance.

AMY. And how often do you perform?

ADRIAN. Regularly.

AMY. $1000 doesn't pay for all this. And you're obviously a man of refined tastes.

ADRIAN. In everything.

AMY. So without your wife's money…

ADRIAN. Precisely.

AMY. How'd you survive before you met her? Or were you willing to do without all these nice things?

ADRIAN. I was never willing to do without anything.

AMY. Then what's the deal?

ADRIAN. You sound like my father. When I was hustling for $5 a game, he used to ask how I intended to support myself playing geeks and wimps.

AMY. What did you tell him?

ADRIAN. How could I say I was waiting for him to die?

AMY. He had money.

(**ADRIAN** *nods.*)

What was he like?

ADRIAN. He was, to borrow from Thomas Hobbes, nasty, brutish, and short. His idea of culture was a cockfight. But he was a drone, and devoted his life to scrounging for income. Fortunately, he was a crooked drone. And through various manipulations in real estate, stocks, and who knows what else, accrued a tidy sum before dropping dead at fifty-eight.

AMY. What about your mother?

ADRIAN. She read the Bible, lit candles, and prayed for my father's soul. When I picture the two of them together, I have no idea why I was conceived. Or how.

AMY. Brothers or sisters?

ADRIAN. I was more than my parents could handle.

AMY. Is your mother alive?

ADRIAN. She died soon after. Hardly anyone noticed.

AMY. Then all your father's money came to you.

ADRIAN. What was left after the government weighed in.

AMY. Nothing.

ADRIAN. Bingo.

AMY. How many years ago was that?

ADRIAN. Ten.

AMY. And you married your wife four years ago.

ADRIAN. You've done your research.

AMY. What happened in between?

ADRIAN. I married someone else.

AMY. How did you meet her?

ADRIAN. A man like me never has trouble meeting women.

AMY. What kind of man is that?

ADRIAN. A man who appreciates the finer things…including women. When women come across such a fellow, they instinctively make themselves available. No matter what his character.

AMY. Tell me about her.

ADRIAN. Mona was…wealthy.

(short pause)

AMY. There must have been more.

ADRIAN. Bovine features, porcine figure. Yet she did have one redeeming quality. Like most girls, she despised her family. And what better way to irritate them then by marrying an attractive man with no means of support.

(a beat)

I'd appreciate if you didn't quote me.

AMY. Only if you tell me what went wrong with the marriage.

ADRIAN. I met Janice. You're sure you don't need a notebook?

AMY. Nope.

ADRIAN. I called that magazine where you said you worked. No one was aware of your employment.

AMY. Did you ask for the Associate Editor? I'm on his private staff.

ADRIAN. Ah. Still, it's surprising that the personnel office had no record of you.

AMY. I just started. My name's probably not in the system yet.

ADRIAN. Where else have you worked?

AMY. I've been free-lancing.

ADRIAN. How many articles have you sold during the past year?

AMY. Not many.

ADRIAN. Exactly how many?

AMY. Exactly none.

ADRIAN. Any prospects for this piece? Do you intend to write any of this down?

(From behind, he strokes her shoulders and hair.)

What do you do?

AMY. (turning to him) What would you like done?

(She walks away.)

ADRIAN. Why are you here?

AMY. The other night I went on a date. Nobody special, but he took me to an extraordinary exhibition by a man with a unique mind. I'd like to know that mind better.

ADRIAN. How'd you get my phone number?

AMY. I asked at the chess club.

ADRIAN. They're not supposed to give it out.

AMY. I asked nicely.

> *(a beat)*

I hear you have your share of women visitors.

ADRIAN. They come. They go.

AMY. I didn't see many women at that chess thing.

ADRIAN. No surprise.

AMY. Not a woman's game?

ADRIAN. There's the occasional mutant freak, but the vast majority play to no consequence whatsoever.

AMY. Any reason? Or just lack of opportunity?

ADRIAN. Lack of imagination. Deficiency of will. No killer instinct.

AMY. You'd be surprised what some women can do.

ADRIAN. Doesn't matter. One of life's amusing ironies is that even if a woman does achieve, she's still…only a woman.

AMY. You really mean that.

ADRIAN. Absolutely. Oh, I know. These days women run marathons and businesses, and they run for office. They pretend to be police officers and soldiers. But they're only parodies of the real thing. After all, once a woman can do something…how impressive can it be?

AMY. What about your wife?

ADRIAN. What about her?

AMY. She's rich, and she's powerful. How does that make you feel?

ADRIAN. There are people in this world who are lucky. I assume you're aware that Janice began as a warm-up girl in a third-rate spa.

AMY. I know the story, but let's hear your version.

ADRIAN. Not much to tell. One morning a talk show needed someone to demonstrate exercises for the beach. Within three weeks, she was a regular. Within two years, she had put out a video and her own line of clothing, and was on her way to being a corporation. A few years later, she met me.

AMY. How did you fit in?

ADRIAN. There are people in this world who are meant to live off people who are lucky.

AMY. What'd she see in you?

ADRIAN. Quite a lot. Remember, I've competed at world-class level. And when you toss in youthful charm and looks...well, I think of myself as an exotic catch.

AMY. And you're happy.

ADRIAN. Don't I look it?

AMY. Then why all the women?

ADRIAN. In a world ruled by the ugly and barbaric, I am a lonely outpost of civility, savoring the best in food, drink, and culture. And women.

AMY. In the meantime your wife struts across the country. Calls you "the little man."

ADRIAN. So I've heard.

AMY. How about "the old balls and chain"?

(a beat)

ADRIAN. That's new.

AMY. No, it isn't.

ADRIAN. Let's say I'm proud of her.

AMY. You're lying. No husband's proud of a wife who leaves him in her dust.

ADRIAN. I get what I want.

AMY. How much does it cost?

ADRIAN. The price is trivial.

AMY. But humiliating. I hear she makes you play by her rules. Tells you how much to spend. I hear you think she's crude and cheap.

ADRIAN. Don't hold anything back.

AMY. People say you're a leech. I see a man who knows he's smart, but whose gifts don't pay. So he has to live off a woman who keeps him on a very tight leash. The question is, when are you going to something about it?

ADRIAN. Divorce? She'd fix it so I end up with nothing.

AMY. There are other ways.

ADRIAN. Why do you care?

AMY. I know her better than you think.

ADRIAN. How much better?

AMY. When I was young…younger, I realized I'd have to depend on my body for a living. You can imagine what I had to do. And who I had to do it with. But a couple of years ago I saw your wife. If she could make it, why not me? So I took a job at her New York club.

ADRIAN. Congratulations.

AMY. I met a guy there. Robert Barnett. Know him?

ADRIAN. I never go to the shop.

AMY. You'd learn a lot.

ADRIAN. For instance.

AMY. That Janice knows Robert, too. In every sense of the word. You think you have plenty of women for your amusement? Trust me. Your wife has more than a couple of men for hers.

ADRIAN. She always comes back to me.

AMY. Only for decoration. You see, Janice wanted Robert all for herself. So one day, when she was screaming her way through the building, she ordered me to put in for a transfer to Atlanta. Told me never to see Robert again.

ADRIAN. Sounds like a threat.

AMY. One week later, the company accused me of selling drugs. And of servicing male clients in ways that were not acceptable.

ADRIAN. All untrue, I presume.

AMY. When they searched my locker, they found pills.

ADRIAN. Stupid to leave them there.

AMY. That's what I told security.

ADRIAN. You figure somebody planted them?

AMY. Somebody? Janice told me she'd drop all charges and avoid bad publicity for me *and* the organization if I went for what she called "treatment." Otherwise…

ADRIAN. Were you on anything?

AMY. I HAD IT UNDER CONTROL!

(The outburst shocks **ADRIAN**. **AMY** *calms herself.)*

I spent four months and thirteen days there.

ADRIAN. Most of those places are practically country clubs.

AMY. This wasn't. Would you like to hear what some of the guards did to me? Just for kicks?

ADRIAN. I get the picture –

AMY. I went through HELL! And I want the woman who put me there to pay for it.

(short pause)

I tried to see Robert, but she's put him out in L.A. He wouldn't take my call.

ADRIAN. Maybe he's the one you should be angry at.

AMY. I want to get 'em both.

ADRIAN. I'm not sure I follow.

AMY. *(moving behind him)* Suddenly you're awfully slow. I bet you think about it all the time. Every time she goose-steps through the doorway. Every time she orders you to cook dinner or clean the bathroom. Every time she prefers a bed in town to yours. Every time she reminds you that she makes the money, that you need her for every meal you eat and every piece of clothing you wear. I figure you imagine waking up one day, and suddenly she's gone. The house is yours. The cars are yours. The business is yours. The bankbook has one name on it.

ADRIAN. You have a vivid imagination.

AMY. I know you.

ADRIAN. You don't know anything about me –

AMY. I know you!

(*short pause*)

ADRIAN. I don't want to talk about it.

AMY. Why not?

ADRIAN. Because it can't happen!

AMY. Happens every day.

ADRIAN. Not to someone like her. This is front-page stuff.

AMY. See? You have thought about it. Now what if I told you that –

ADRIAN. That's enough.

AMY. All I was going to say is that –

ADRIAN. Stop it! I'm willing to do a lot to keep what I have. But you're going too far.

AMY. Would it make any difference if I told you she's hired a new lawyer? A divorce lawyer? Have you checked her will lately? How much is left in *your* name?

ADRIAN. How do you know all this?

AMY. Everybody knows!

(*short pause*)

You could kill her ten different ways. With your talent for strategy, I'm sure you can think of something.

(*He reflects, then laughs.*)

ADRIAN. This is crazy!

AMY. Is it?

ADRIAN. It can't be done!

AMY. Happens every day.

ADRIAN. Stop saying that!

(*short pause*)

Look, even if everything…worked out, what's in it for you?

AMY. Beside revenge? Afterwards you'll have enough to spare something for a close friend. Say $100,000.

ADRIAN. What about Barnett?

AMY. When you get the company, fire him. Then I'll take over.

(**ADRIAN** *looks at her and reflects, then shakes his head.*)

ADRIAN. Too risky.

AMY. Why?

ADRIAN. Only one thing has to go wrong!

AMY. Only a few things have to go right. How long can you stand her?

ADRIAN. You mean how long can I live with Attila the Hunnette?

AMY. I never heard anybody call her that.

ADRIAN. That's mine.

AMY. You dream about killing her. Don't you want to do it? Or has she cut off everything?

ADRIAN. Watch it!

AMY. You'd be getting back at all the women like her. With the designer suits and the power breakfasts.

ADRIAN. The ones who smile, then grind their heels into you.

(*short pause*)

I know *how* I'd do it.

AMY. Go on.

ADRIAN. In art, simplicity is best. First something in a drink. Enough to make her dizzy. Then take her upstairs. Fill the tub with water. Knock her head against the side. Put her in. And under. Wait fifteen minutes. Then call the police.

(*pathetic tone*)

I was downstairs, officer. I didn't know she had taken pills. I didn't hear her fall. I didn't hear a thing. She just died.

(*normal tone*)

How sad. How ironic. A woman with all her athletic talent slips in the bathtub and dies.

AMY. I want to help.

ADRIAN. I don't need you.

AMY. You do now.

ADRIAN. Am I really going to do this?

(*pause*)

I could use a conveniently placed witness.

AMY. Let's hear it.

ADRIAN. When the police come, you're here. You tell them that you arrived earlier. That Janice called for you. She knew about your troubles and wanted to help a former employee. Before she went upstairs, she promised you a new job. And a loan to get you back on your feet.

AMY. Do I get either one?

ADRIAN. Not then. You claim that I was down here with you the whole time, that I didn't want Janice to give you a dime. Let 'em know that you despise me. Call me every name in the book.

AMY. So they don't think that we're together.

ADRIAN. Exactly.

AMY. Leech.

ADRIAN. Parasite.

AMY. All-American creep. Two-bit hustler. Greedy, slimy –

ADRIAN. You've grasped the concept. Between your tears over Janice and your disgust with me, you confirm my story. Then I'm in the clear. Later I send you the money.

AMY. $100,000.

ADRIAN. Double it. Charming, isn't it?

AMY. I love it. When?

(*She kisses him. He responds, then stares at her.*)

ADRIAN. You're serious, aren't you?

AMY. Aren't you? *When?* Or do *you* lack killer instinct?

(*He looks at her, then shakes his head and moves away.*)

ADRIAN. I can't do it!

AMY. Let me put it this way. I don't know how long it's
going to take. Maybe a few weeks. Maybe more. But
she's fed up with you. You'll be out with the trash. Got
any rich friends? Feel like beggin' 'em for a few bucks?
You might even have to go to work. But what could
you do? And even if you find something, you'll end up
living in a dump somewhere. You'll be lucky to have
one lousy bottle of sherry.

(short pause)

I don't think you have a choice. If you want to keep all
this, you have to get rid of her. The good news is, you
know how.

(long pause)

ADRIAN. She comes back from Chicago tomorrow.

AMY. What time?

(She draws close.)

You're gonna do it. Yes, you are.

(She kisses him.)

Sexy, isn't it?

ADRIAN. The outfit? I told you. I like it –

AMY. I'm talking about murder.

ADRIAN. The thought is arousing.

AMY. Then do we seal the deal?

ADRIAN. What's on your mind?

AMY. You've got to be kidding!

*(She begins to unbutton his shirt. He stops her and
moves away.)*

ADRIAN. Don't hurry. Let's play with the idea. Seems to me
that two imaginative people ought to create a scenario
that makes the entire enterprise more stimulating.

AMY. I'm listening.

ADRIAN. The moment you walked in, I was certain that you
were one of those rare women who enjoy holding a
man's attention by the simple act of removing their
clothing. Slowly. Piece by piece.

(He sits opposite her. **AMY** *removes one shoe. He snaps his fingers and extends his hand. She tosses the shoe to him. She removes her other shoe and tosses it to him.)*

(She starts to unbutton her blouse.)

End of Scene 3

Scene 4

(Two afternoons later.)

*(**JANICE** enters, barefoot and wearing a robe over a swim-suit. She goes to the bar and pours a drink.)*

*(A moment later, **AMY** follows, dressed in street clothes. She carries her shoes, which she drops by the door.)*

JANICE. Drink?

AMY. Maybe later.

(a beat)

I like the way you keep in shape.

JANICE. Nothing scares men more than a woman who's secure about her own body. When I strut in, the game's practically over.

AMY. I like your style, too.

JANICE. The subject is my husband.

AMY. Where should I start?

JANICE. I want every detail.

AMY. First tell me one thing. What did you ever see in him?

JANICE. The same thing every woman sees. The brains, the looks, and the charm. The problem was what came later. What you saw the other day.

AMY. What about his first wife?

JANICE. *(contemptuous)* Mona?

AMY. Did you feel sorry for her?

JANICE. I don't feel sorry for any woman who lets herself be used.

AMY. Should I take that personally?

JANICE. You'll be paid. Last I heard, she had a breakdown. They put her away somewhere.

AMY. The first Mrs. Bonham.

JANICE. The only one. I never have been, and never will be, Mrs. Anybody. Tell me everything.

AMY. I showed up in the middle of the afternoon, dressed like you told me. And you were right. He likes skirts and heels.

JANICE. Hates pants. I wonder why.

AMY. It was a couple of days after the chess thing. His time to strut.

JANICE. I'm sure he did.

AMY. I told him I was a reporter.

JANICE. How long did he buy it?

AMY. Not very. I let him see through me quickly. Anyway, his mind was on other things.

JANICE. You're a woman. And a pretty one.

AMY. Thanks.

(**JANICE** *goes to her desk and writes a check.*)

JANICE. First he offered you a drink, right? Brandy?

AMY. Sherry.

JANICE. Along with a poetic description of its superior qualities.

AMY. He couldn't wait to tell me about himself. First his family.

JANICE. Which variation?

AMY. How many are there?

JANICE. Sometimes he insists he worked himself up. Rambles on about two jobs to support his brother and sister.

AMY. Not this time.

JANICE. Did he tell you he was adopted?

AMY. Was he?

JANICE. Of course not. But he figures that women'll get weepy over a story of poverty, so he gives them the Oliver Twist plot. How he stayed up all night, studying chess by the dim glow of one flickering bulb. Heartbreaking stuff.

AMY. He told me about his father, the crooked drone who dropped dead…

JANICE. With the mother lighting candles and saying prayers.

AMY. That's it.

JANICE. Good God, he told you the truth.

AMY. It sounded legit.

JANICE. He took right to you.

AMY. I'm not sure that's a compliment.

JANICE. I'm not sure it was meant to be.

(JANICE gives the check to AMY, who tucks it in her blouse.)

AMY. He went out of his way to insult you. And women in general.

JANICE. He doesn't dare talk that way when I'm around. But when one of his playmates shows up, it all spews out. At least that's what I've suspected. How'd he get you into bed?

(short pause)

AMY. You sure you want to know everything?

JANICE. What was the game?

AMY. I had to strip.

JANICE. He loves giving women orders. How far did you go?

AMY. Part of the way. Then he took over. First on the floor. There.

(She points.)

JANICE. First?

AMY. Then upstairs.

JANICE. He's not usually so energetic.

(She goes for a drink.)

AMY. I guess I brought out his best.

(Unseen by AMY, JANICE clenches in anger but maintains control.)

Wasn't I supposed to go all the way?

JANICE. If you had to.

AMY. Why don't you just divorce him?

JANICE. He still has too much in his name. And I've worked too hard to let a sponger like that have anything.

AMY. I can tell you what he wants.

JANICE. What?

AMY. Everything.

JANICE. What's he gonna do? Kill me?

> (JANICE *laughs.* AMY *does not.*)

> What did he say?

AMY. He didn't come right out with it. First I told him our story. How you fired me and that I was out for revenge. At that point he was curious, but not convinced.

JANICE. What changed his mind?

AMY. When I told him that you had hired a new lawyer. Finally, *finally*, he admitted that he had a plan.

JANICE. This ought to be good.

AMY. An accident in the bathroom. You hit your head, then drown in the tub.

JANICE. That's all? I'm surprised he didn't come up with something more sophisticated. Does he figure he can do it alone?

AMY. He says he could. Although I volunteered to help.

> (JANICE *looks at her.*)

> Thought I'd better remove any doubt.

JANICE. Sounds like you carried off everything perfectly. In fact, you're everything dear Bobby Barnett said you were.

AMY. He knows women. Do you miss him?

JANICE. He's not worth pining over.

AMY. I know that now. But back then...you could've had any man you wanted. Why'd you pick mine?

JANICE. For the same reason you wanted him. He did the job.

AMY. And very well. Maybe because that's all he was good for. But I couldn't compete with you.

JANICE. I wouldn't say that.

AMY. You're beautiful, you're smart, and you're rich.

JANICE. How generous.

AMY. When I lost Bobby, I went crazy. Started drinking. Got back into drugs. In a few more weeks, I would've been back on the street.

JANICE. That's why I arranged for you to get help.

AMY. It was rough.

JANICE. I'm sure.

AMY. But you did the right thing. Bobby couldn't have done it. He's too weak.

JANICE. That's why I sent him packing. To do what he does best. With anyone who'll have him.

AMY. You couldn't trust him. You can't trust any of them. That's what I like about women. Deep down, we're stronger.

JANICE. And tougher. When we want to be.

AMY. I know. I've heard people call you vicious.

JANICE. So have I.

AMY. Cold. Bitchy. Vengeful –

JANICE. And those are my friends.

AMY. You've got guts, that's all. You knew what you wanted, and you went out and got it.

JANICE. But I paid for it. I never know who I can trust. That's what I find comforting about Adrian. I know he's using me. And of course I'm using him.

AMY. Wouldn't it be more comforting to have someone you really care for? Someone you *can* trust?

JANICE. I haven't met the man.

AMY. Who said anything about men?

(short pause)

You need someone understanding, who sees things *your* way.

JANICE. What are you suggesting?

(**AMY** *draws very close to* **JANICE.**)

AMY. Can I have that drink now?

(**JANICE** *goes to the bar.*)

I promised him I'd support his story about your death.

(**JANICE** *picks up a bottle.* **AMY** *walks to the bar.*)

I'd much rather support your story about his.

(**JANICE** *stares at her.* **AMY** *stands right next to her.*)

We could say that he was drinking too much. That he must have fallen and hit his head, then drowned in the bathtub. Or the pool.

(**JANICE** *pours two drinks. She holds out one to* **AMY,** *who takes it.* **JANICE.** *picks up her own.*)

(*They touch glasses, then sip their drinks.*)

Sexy, isn't it?

End of Act I

ACT II

Scene 1

(The next evening.)

*(**JANICE** lies on the couch, reading.)*

*(**ADRIAN** enters holding a knife, and stares at her, then slowly walks to her. When he is next to her, he turns and puts the knife on the bar.)*

ADRIAN. I've been thinking.

JANICE. Yes?

ADRIAN. About the Palm Beach apartment. Maybe we should sell it. No use throwing away money.

JANICE. Funny. I was thinking just the opposite. You made some good points the other night.

(He kisses her intensely.)

What was that for?

ADRIAN. Just my way of saying that whatever minor squabbles we have, I happen to be completely in love with you.

JANICE. What more could a woman want to hear?

ADRIAN. I hope you feel the same way.

JANICE. You're still the most stimulating man I've ever met.

ADRIAN. And who can resist that?

(short pause)

As long as we're doing so well, I suppose I can bring up an awkward subject.

JANICE. What's that?

ADRIAN. I had a visitor the other day.

JANICE. Here?

ADRIAN. Hm-mm. A woman.

JANICE. Of course.

ADRIAN. This is serious.

JANICE. Pardon me. Someone I know?

ADRIAN. I believe so. She said she was –

JANICE. Don't tell me. A model.

(**ADRIAN** *shakes his head.*)

An actress. A prospective trainer.

ADRIAN. I think she used to work for you.

JANICE. In one of the clubs?

ADRIAN. That's what she said.

JANICE. Hardly narrows it down. Can you be more specific?

ADRIAN. Awfully pretty.

JANICE. Most of them are.

ADRIAN. Wonderful smile. Firm, shapely body.

JANICE. As I said, most of them –

ADRIAN. And she claimed you nearly had her arrested.

JANICE. Amy Courtland.

ADRIAN. Got it on the first try.

JANICE. I was hoping I was wrong. How'd she get here?

ADRIAN. She just dropped by.

JANICE. To see me?

ADRIAN. No.

JANICE. Had you ever met her?

ADRIAN. No.

JANICE. Then what was she doing here?

ADRIAN. I don't know where to start.

JANICE. Try the beginning.

ADRIAN. Okay. She called and told me she was a reporter. Said she'd like to interview me.

JANICE. How'd she get the number?

ADRIAN. She said she asked at the club, but I don't think so.

JANICE. Did she say why she picked you?

ADRIAN. She told me she happened to be at my last exhibition –

JANICE. Happened to be?

ADRIAN. Someone took her.

JANICE. Someone?

ADRIAN. Do you want to know what she said?

JANICE. Go ahead.

ADRIAN. She claimed that she was so impressed by my performance that I might be worthy of a magazine article.

JANICE. You would be a fascinating subject.

ADRIAN. Thank you. But that particular story didn't hold. I saw right through it.

JANICE. Clever of you.

ADRIAN. Not really. She made it obvious she was lying, that she wanted me to expose her. So to speak.

JANICE. Then what happened?

ADRIAN. She told me she used to work for you. That you were her inspiration.

JANICE. I've heard that before.

ADRIAN. She then went on about someone named Robert Barnett. Claimed they were in love.

JANICE. Oh, God.

ADRIAN. But apparently somebody interfered.

JANICE. Don't tell me. I'm responsible for the collapse of her love life.

ADRIAN. She said you wanted Barnett for yourself.

JANICE. *I* wanted *him?*

ADRIAN. That's what she said.

JANICE. She's a liar!

ADRIAN. I told her I didn't believe her. But she insisted.

JANICE. Delusions.

ADRIAN. That's what I thought. Why would she concoct such a wild fantasy? Then she told me that you threatened her. That you screamed at her to quit her job and get out.

JANICE. I DON'T...

> (short pause)

I don't scream.

ADRIAN. I know! Then came the most incredible part. She claims that you planted drugs in her locker, then accused her of selling them. Then...and this is the craziest thing...you accused her of being a hooker and using the club to promote business!

JANICE. You're kidding!

ADRIAN. That's what she said.

JANICE. She gets nuttier all the time.

ADRIAN. Then you had her put away.

JANICE. For two months.

ADRIAN. Four.

JANICE. Whatever! Apparently it didn't do any good. You should have thrown her out.

ADRIAN. I was tempted, believe me.

JANICE. What stopped you?

ADRIAN. I knew she had a reason for handing me this pack of lies. I wanted to hear it.

JANICE. Did you?

ADRIAN. Hold on. She told me that you're planning to divorce me.

JANICE. Why would she –

ADRIAN. There's more! She knew everything about our personal lives. Our most intimate affairs.

JANICE. Sounds like she's been sneaking all over the place.

ADRIAN. A bit spooky, let me tell you. I decided the best thing was to pretend I was intrigued. That's why I said I was angry with you. In fact, I put on an entire act about how I don't like women.

JANICE. You not like women?

ADRIAN. I brought it off. Then came the kicker: she wants me to kill you.

> (JANICE looks at him.)

ADRIAN. *(continued)* That's it? Just a stare? Not even an expression of controlled outrage?

JANICE. I'm waiting for details.

ADRIAN. She suggested an accident around the house.

JANICE. What did you say?

ADRIAN. What do you think?

JANICE. I want to hear.

ADRIAN. I went along. Just to see how far she'd go.

JANICE. And how far was that?

ADRIAN. She started to take off her clothes. Right there.

(He gestures.)

JANICE. Right there?

(She touches a specific spot. He touches a spot inches away.)

ADRIAN. Right *there.*

JANICE. And how did you respond?

ADRIAN. What do you think?

JANICE. I think you nailed her.

(She points to the spot **ADRIAN** *designated.)*

Right there.

ADRIAN. Why would you think that?

JANICE. Because that's what Amy told me. I sent her here.

(Pause. **ADRIAN** *kisses* **JANICE.***)*

ADRIAN. I know.

*(***JANICE** *stares at him. He smiles smugly.)*

I knew it the whole time. Even before she showed up, I could see your hand in it.

JANICE. I don't believe you.

ADRIAN. Her name wasn't at the magazine she was supposed to work for. She couldn't remember any articles she had written. When she tried to take notes, she didn't have a pen. I'm surprised you couldn't find someone more...polished.

JANICE. You seem to have found her attractive enough.

ADRIAN. I suppose she's good-looking. In a cheap way. But all I did was play my part. Just to see how far she'd go. Or how far you told her to go.

JANICE. And how far was that?

ADRIAN. A little necking in the parlor.

JANICE. You're lying! You did it in our bed. She told me!

ADRIAN. Oh, she wanted to. But I couldn't do that to you. Even if you did set me up.

JANICE. Why would she lie?

ADRIAN. You may not want to hear this. You may not believe it. But this girl has it in for you.

JANICE. I saved her life! She was a druggie, sleeping with anybody for a fix! I even got her away from that slime Barnett.

ADRIAN. She doesn't think so. She blames you for breaking up her romance and dumping her in the loony bin. Now she figures she's recruited me to do a job on you.

JANICE. Why didn't you just turn her down?

ADRIAN. Because she'd find someone else. Whatever she's told you, forget it. You think you were using *her* to check on *me*? She wants to use *me* to get rid of *you*. She wants you dead, Janice.

(*a beat*)

Tell me about Robert Barnett.

JANICE. There's nothing to tell.

ADRIAN. Tell me about nothing.

JANICE. You think I'd bother with a glorified towel boy?

ADRIAN. Tell me.

JANICE. I amused myself by leading him on. That's it.

ADRIAN. Where is he now?

JANICE. California.

ADRIAN. Still working for you?

JANICE. Don't be ridiculous.

ADRIAN. Think he carries a grudge?

JANICE. What are you getting at?

ADRIAN. Just looking a few moves ahead. How did you locate Amy this time?

JANICE. I didn't. She came to my office and said she needed work.

ADRIAN. I want the truth.

JANICE. That's what happened! She showed up and said she'd do anything for me.

ADRIAN. But she knew you wouldn't hire her. You couldn't! Not at one of your places.

JANICE. Then why did she come?

ADRIAN. Which one of you mentioned me first?

JANICE. She did.

ADRIAN. How much did she know?

JANICE. Rumors I'd heard before. I was curious if they were true.

ADRIAN. Then it was your idea to set up this charade.

JANICE. No, it was hers. She knew all about the chess match, so she offered to go, then call you up.

ADRIAN. How did she know about it?

JANICE. She didn't say.

ADRIAN. Did she ask for money?

JANICE. No.

ADRIAN. Did she ask for anything in return?

JANICE. No.

ADRIAN. Nothing?

JANICE. She said she wanted to repay me for helping her. Wanted to do me a favor.

ADRIAN. A favor.

JANICE. That's what she said.

ADRIAN. And you believed her?

JANICE. I did the other day.

ADRIAN. You're not usually so gullible.

JANICE. She caught me off guard.

ADRIAN. She does have a plaintive, soulful quality.

JANICE. Did she tell you she once tried to kill a client?

ADRIAN. No.

JANICE. Maybe "kill" is too strong a word. But she did try to crush his skull with a ten-pound weight. Claimed he attacked her in the steam room.

ADRIAN. Why am I growing less comfortable with this person roaming free on the planet?

JANICE. Then you won't be surprised to learn that she's ready to kill you, too.

ADRIAN. Did she say that?

JANICE. Hm-mm.

ADRIAN. How does she plan to do it?

JANICE. The same way you two were going to get rid of me.

ADRIAN. Not only is she a murderer. She's a plagiarist.

JANICE. Is it our turn to switch the game on her?

ADRIAN. Let's face it. This girl is dangerous. And even if she doesn't become violent, who knows where she'll show up next? She could go to the papers or television. She could humiliate us.

(short pause)

JANICE. She could do a lot worse than that.

ADRIAN. What do you mean?

JANICE. About a year ago, Barnett was in on some financial moves I made.

ADRIAN. What kind of moves?

JANICE. With company stock.

ADRIAN. Legal?

JANICE. Not exactly.

ADRIAN. I knew it! Didn't I tell you?

JANICE. Will you forget that? I'm not worried about Barnett, because he knows that if he talks, he'll go to jail. But Amy has nothing to lose. And if he told her even half of what he knows, and she spills it, she could bring the company down. Right on our heads.

(pause)

ADRIAN. I'm going to invite her here tomorrow night.

JANICE. Why?

ADRIAN. Which answer do you want? The one I give her? Or the real one?

JANICE. Both.

ADRIAN. I'm telling *her* that we're going along with her plan, that we're going to kill *you*. I'm telling *you* that we're going to dispose of *her*.

JANICE. You sound awfully cold-blooded.

ADRIAN. Thank you, Lady Macbeth. Look, you and I may have our problems, but we are also exceptional people who deserve an exceptional partner. Agreed?

JANICE. Agreed.

ADRIAN. Ms. Courtland, on the other hand, is not of our element. She is coarse and stupid. Tomorrow night when she arrives, she sees us together. She realizes that her masquerade is over, that you and I are a team. We lay matters on the line. We want her out of our lives. While she ponders that ultimatum, we all have a drink. She has a great deal to drink, with something extra tossed in.

JANICE. She may not take anything.

ADRIAN. We insist. Physically, if necessary.

(a beat)

I'll hold. You pour.

(a beat)

Then we put her in her car. She drives off, blotto. She speeds. She swerves. She crashes. The end.

JANICE. Suppose someone knows she was here.

(short pause)

ADRIAN. Suppose someone does? Our story is simple. She came here drunk. And who knows what else? With her history, no one would be surprised. You welcomed her with sympathy and offered to recommend her to a competitor. She demanded money. You refused. She made threats, then left. We recognized her condition and tried to keep her here, but she sped off down the road. That's the last we saw of her.

JANICE. We did all we could.

ADRIAN. We're compassionate people.

JANICE. You're sure you can make the drinks strong enough? We don't want any recoveries.

(**ADRIAN** *walks to the bar.* **JANICE** *follows.*)

ADRIAN. I know an especially virulent variety of xanax, one Mona used to gulp in weaker moments. The doctors warned us how dangerous it can be, particularly when mixed with alcohol. The combination is lethal. I'll pack Amy's drink. Before long, she's almost out. Before much longer, even if she manages to stop the car, she's out permanently.

(*He fills two glasses and offers one to* **JANICE**, *who takes it.*)

What do you say?

JANICE. I say we eliminate her.

ADRIAN. Whom God hath brought together…

JANICE. …let no one put asunder.

(*They clink glasses and smile.*)

End of Scene 1

Scene 2

(The next evening.)

(The top of the bar is empty of all bottles.)

*(**JANICE** paces nervously. **ADRIAN** enters and strolls to the bar, where he pours a drink from a carafe.)*

JANICE. What time is it?

ADRIAN. She'll be here.

JANICE. I want her out of our lives.

ADRIAN. Won't be long.

JANICE. Who's going to answer the door?

ADRIAN. Why so nervous?

JANICE. Just being careful. I didn't get where I am without planning every step.

ADRIAN. I can say the same thing about myself.

(short pause)

Did I tell you I heard from Felicia Cromwell? She found that new tapestry. The one with the medieval pattern –

JANICE. Will you forget the damn tapestry?

ADRIAN. Sorry.

(a beat)

But I would like to give her a bonus. She's worked hard and –

(She glares at him. He holds up a hand in apology, then moves to embrace her.)

Not another word. All a-dither, aren't you?

JANICE. We're about to kill someone. We'll decorate later.

ADRIAN. Whatever you say. May I suggest that when she comes, you should be out of the room. She expects to ally herself with me. Let's not frighten the girl.

JANICE. That's the least of my concerns.

ADRIAN. You think she'll be tough?

JANICE. I wouldn't be surprised.

>   *(She turns quickly.)*

>   What's that?

>   (**ADRIAN** *peers out a window.*)

ADRIAN. She's here. Give me a moment with her.

>   (**JANICE** *hesitates, then leaves.* **ADRIAN** *walks offstage.*
>   **AMY** *enters, wearing a blouse, a flared skirt, and heels.*
>   **ADRIAN** *follows.*)

ADRIAN. *(continued)* And how are you?

AMY. Eager. Where is she?

ADRIAN. She'll be right down.

AMY. Good.

>   *(She laughs and kisses him. He breaks away.)*

ADRIAN. Later!

AMY. Nervous?

ADRIAN. Shhh!

>   (**AMY** *laughs.* **JANICE** *enters.*)

JANICE. I thought I heard a familiar giggle.

AMY. Janice! It's wonderful to see you.

>   *(They hug.)*

JANICE. Sorry I couldn't be here the other night.

AMY. I understand. You're always on the move.

JANICE. How are you feeling?

AMY. Coming along.

JANICE. Those must have been painful weeks.

AMY. Months.

JANICE. Yet sometimes the difficult experiences give us the strength to carry on.

AMY. I'm trying to look at it as a positive thing.

ADRIAN. Wouldn't you two be more comfortable sitting?

>   (**JANICE** *and* **AMY** *look at each other, then sit on the couch.*)

ADRIAN. *(continued)* There you go! Now…

JANICE. How are you spending your time?

AMY. For the moment, getting readjusted is tough enough.

JANICE. Looking for a job?

ADRIAN. No, I'm keeping busy. But thanks for asking.

JANICE. I was speaking to Amy.

ADRIAN. Oh!

AMY. Checking every opportunity.

JANICE. I gather journalism didn't work out.

AMY. I'm more of a people person.

JANICE. Well, if I can be of any help…

AMY. I don't want to impose.

JANICE. I understand. Anyway, I'm sure you'll get a break soon enough.

ADRIAN. Probably one right around the corner. Ever consider looking out West?

JANICE. Why would she?

ADRIAN. New places, new faces.

AMY. I admit I wouldn't mind getting away from here.

ADRIAN. What a coincidence! Janice is heading out to California next week. You know anybody out there, Amy?

AMY. A few people.

ADRIAN. You two probably have friends in common. In the fitness biz.

JANICE. Would you like me to check around the clubs? There might be a spot for you.

ADRIAN. Great idea.

JANICE. I asked Amy.

AMY. It is the field I know best.

ADRIAN. And Janice has plenty of contacts.

JANICE. I'll see what I can do.

ADRIAN. Things are looking up already! But I've been rude. Amy, care for a drink?

AMY. Only if everybody else is having something.

ADRIAN. We'll all join in.

(*He examines the bottles under the bar.*)

Not from this batch, though. Why don't I check the *specialité de la maison*?

AMY. Don't go to trouble on my account.

ADRIAN. Not at all! Nothing I enjoy more than rummaging through the vaults and finding a treasure for my guests.

(*He pats* **AMY**'s hand.)

JANICE. Then why don't you?

AMY. It's a very sweet gesture.

ADRIAN. That's me all over.

(*Smiling,* **ADRIAN** *leaves. When he is out of sight,* **AMY** *takes from her bag a short, thick club.*)

AMY. When do you want it done?

JANICE. As soon as possible.

AMY. And then?

JANICE. Out to the pool. We'll drown him there.

(**AMY** *nods, then replaces the club.* **ADRIAN** *returns with a bottle.*)

ADRIAN. Here we are!

(*He shows them the bottle.*)

Chenin Blanc. The perfect summertime aperitif. Is that acceptable to you girls?

(*a beat*)

Pardon me. *Ladies? Women?*

AMY. I'm just a guest.

JANICE. Who are we to challenge the judgment of an expert?

ADRIAN. How flattering! Shall I pour?

(*He goes to the bar and opens the bottle.*)

AMY. Only a drop for me. I have to drive back.

ADRIAN. A couple of sips can't hurt.

AMY. I guess not. Oh, pardon me. Where's the bathroom?

JANICE. *(pointing)* Second door on your right.

AMY. Thanks.

> *(She and **JANICE** exchange smiles. As **AMY** leaves, **ADRIAN** glances at her, and she nods in return. When **AMY** is out of sight, **JANICE** hurries to him)*

JANICE. Now what?

ADRIAN. We wait.

> *(He shows her the bottle.)*

> See what I did?

JANICE. What are you talking about?

ADRIAN. You can't tell, can you?

> *(**ADRIAN** and **JANICE** have their backs to the door through which **AMY** left.)*

JANICE. What is it?

> *(**JANICE** looks closer. As she does, **AMY** enters silently, shoeless and carrying the club.)*

ADRIAN. After I fixed the bottle, I spread dust back over it. You can't tell a thing.

JANICE. Brilliant. But what difference does it make?

> *(**AMY** is close behind them. She raises the club.)*

ADRIAN. I hated to ruin even so modest a treat, but I think the prize is worthwhile.

> *(**AMY** smashes the club into **JANICE**'s head. **JANICE** groans and collapses, unconscious. **ADRIAN** stands frozen.)*

AMY. Okay! Let's go to work!

ADRIAN. *What–!?*

AMY. Don't stand there!

ADRIAN. But what did you *do*!?

AMY. Exactly what we planned! Now do you have the guts to finish her off? Or do I have to do that, too?

(She forces the club into his hand.)

ADRIAN. Shouldn't we wait?

AMY. For what? Thanksgiving?

ADRIAN. Don't be funny!

AMY. C'mon!

(**ADRIAN** *stares at* **JANICE.**)

What are you doing?

ADRIAN. Thinking!

AMY. About what?

ADRIAN. If this is the only way!

AMY. Are you nuts?

ADRIAN. I'm just trying to figure out if…

AMY. If WHAT!!

ADRIAN. If we can avoid actually killing her!

AMY. It's a little late to think about that now!

ADRIAN. But if there's any way –

AMY. There isn't! If she ends up alive, we're finished!

ADRIAN. But what about the police?

AMY. They won't be able to do anything!

(Right to his face.)

Remember the story! She had too much to drink. She went upstairs, hit her head, and drowned! You were downstairs with me, and you didn't hear a thing –

ADRIAN. Wait a minute! WAIT A MINUTE –

(**ADRIAN** *breaks free and tosses the club aside. She rushes after him and grabs him.*)

AMY. You can't wait! The house, the cars, the business, everything'll be yours! But you have to do it!

ADRIAN. But even if we get away with it –

AMY. We *will* get away with it!

ADRIAN. EVEN IF WE DO…everybody's going to think I murdered my wife!

AMY. Since when do you care what everybody thinks?

(She tightens her grip on him.)

Every man in the country'll say you're a hero. Usually the woman ends up with the goodies. This time you walk away a winner.

ADRIAN. Are you sure we can –

AMY. You can get it all! But you can't wait!

(intense)

Besides, women love dangerous men. You think you're doing well now? Baby, after this, any woman you want.

(He reflects.)

ADRIAN. Let's do it.

AMY. Great! You carry her upstairs! I'll start the water.

*(**ADRIAN** bends over **JANICE**, who stirs.)*

She's beginning to come to! I'll have to hit her again!

*(**ADRIAN** struggles to pull **JANICE** up. He cannot lift her.)*

Stop fooling around!

ADRIAN. She's heavy!

AMY. God, you're pathetic!

ADRIAN. Help me, will you?

AMY. Why don't you get some exercise?

*(They lift **JANICE**.)*

ADRIAN. Will you just –

AMY. C'mon!

*(They start to drag **JANICE** off).*

C'MON!!

End of Scene 2

Scene 3

(*Moments later.*)

(**ADRIAN** *staggers into the room. He struggles to catch his breath.*)

(*He goes to the bar and takes the bottle he showed* **JANICE**. *He is about to drink the poison when he realizes what's in the bottle. Terrified, he yelps and hurriedly puts down the bottle.*)

(*He takes a carafe of wine and swallows.*)

(**AMY** *enters, carrying her shoes and bag. She tosses her shoes on the floor and her bag on the couch.*)

AMY. All done.

(*She looks at* **ADRIAN**, *who hangs onto the bar for support.*)

You okay?

ADRIAN. I don't know!

AMY. Scary, isn't it?

ADRIAN. Definitely!

AMY. But exciting, right?

ADRIAN. I'm not sure that's the word!

AMY. Fulfilling? Satisfying? What would you call it?

(**AMY** *walks to the couch and sits.*)

ADRIAN. Scary will do.

(*a beat*)

I couldn't do it! I just couldn't do it!

(**AMY** *takes out a make-up case and begins to do her face.*)

AMY. Conscience get to you?

ADRIAN. Maybe.

AMY. Once you have the money, you'll get over it.

ADRIAN. I'll keep that thought in mind. Was it hard?

AMY. She bobbed up and down for a while –

ADRIAN. *(wincing)* Geez!

AMY. Maybe she had a vague idea what was happening. But then she stayed under. Good thing you weren't any slower carrying her up the stairs.

ADRIAN. Look, a dead weight's not easy to…God, I didn't think it'd be so tough!

(He sits on a chair.)

AMY. Funny. I found it easier than I expected.

(He stares at her. She finishes her makeup and puts away her case.)

ADRIAN. How long before we call the police?

AMY. Ten, fifteen minutes. Then we can say that we were outside walking, came back, and found her.

(She stands behind him and embraces him.)

ADRIAN. Unconscious.

AMY. Dead.

ADRIAN. I'll say she had been exercising. That's why she needed the bath.

AMY. Aren't you clever.

ADRIAN. And I'm left alone to mourn.

AMY. Just you and your millions.

ADRIAN. And your 200 grand.

AMY. You betcha.

ADRIAN. Is money any substitute for love? That'll be my story.

AMY. You'll recover.

ADRIAN. After an appropriate interval.

(She kisses him.)

Okay. I'm set.

AMY. Very impressive.

ADRIAN. What do we do now?

AMY. *(lying on the couch)* What's on your mind?

ADRIAN. You sure you should stick around?

AMY. That's what we agreed.

ADRIAN. I wonder.

AMY. Are you wondering again?

ADRIAN. Is that the best move?

AMY. Why wouldn't it be?

ADRIAN. Maybe the whole thing'll be more convincing if I'm here alone.

AMY. If I'm here, we can confirm each other's story. That sounds convincing to me.

ADRIAN. You and who else?

AMY. Come again?

ADRIAN. You didn't think up this scheme by yourself.

AMY. Of course not. You helped.

ADRIAN. No, not me. The other night Janice told me everything. That the two of you were working together. That's why you came here the first time.

AMY. Does it matter? She's dead.

ADRIAN. I'd just like to understand what's been happening. Of course, I was sure something was up when you walked in. That nonsense about being a journalist. Writing about a chessplayer. You didn't expect me to believe that.

AMY. No.

ADRIAN. *(standing over her)* But after Janice gave me her side, I knew you didn't go to her office by coincidence. Someone else told you to go. Someone else wanted her dead. How much credit do we give the infamous Mr. Barnett?

AMY. What about him?

ADRIAN. You don't really want him fired, do you?

(He straddles her and grabs her hair.)

Do you?

AMY. No!

ADRIAN. *(pressing her down)* He doesn't have an official job any more, but he lives off the L.A. office, doesn't he?

And once you leave here, you'll join up with him, right? He's probably in line for a good-sized part of the business. And maybe he'll share it with you.

(He releases her.)

I knew sex had to be at the bottom of it. Well, it's a big pie. Plenty of pieces for everyone. But you shouldn't be here when the police come. It'll be easier for one person to maintain a consistent story.

AMY. You sure you can handle it? A few minutes ago you didn't look very confident.

ADRIAN. I can talk better alone.

AMY. *(standing)* Well…?

ADRIAN. What?

AMY. My money.

ADRIAN. I can't give it to you now. When the time's right, I'll send it to you.

AMY. You expect me to believe you?

(He strokes her face.)

ADRIAN. If we can't trust each other, who can we trust? Let's drink on it.

AMY. I still have to drive.

ADRIAN. *(going to the bar)* Just as an expression of good faith. Besides, it's a special bottle. Not to be savored alone.

*(He is at the bar, his back to **AMY**. As he pours a drink from the poisoned bottle, **AMY** reaches underneath her skirt to reveal a knife strapped to her leg. She pulls out the knife, and keeps it from his sight.)*

*(**ADRIAN** turns from the bar, carrying the glass, which is nearly full. She takes it.)*

AMY. That's a good-sized swig.

ADRIAN. These are our final moments together. Let's make them memorable.

*(As he turns away, **AMY** puts down the glass, whirls, and drives the knife into **ADRIAN**'s back.)*

(He screams and falls to the floor.)

ADRIAN. *(continued)* WHY!?

AMY. They'll find you dead. Then they'll find Janice. And
there'll be only one answer. Especially after they inves-
tigate and learn about your indiscretions.

*(He tries to stand, but she kicks him in the back. He
screams in pain. She takes a cell phone from her bag and
dials.)*

She killed you in a rage, then went upstairs to wash off
the blood. And so on, and so on, and so on.

ADRIAN. *(gasping)* They'll get you!

AMY. Why would they even look for me?

(into the phone)

Hi!

ADRIAN. *(in fury and agony)* BARNETT!!

(AMY puts the phone to **ADRIAN**'s ear.)

AMY. It's for you.

ADRIAN. *(breathlessly)* Listen…listen to me…you'll never get
away with it –

(short pause)

What?

(He cries out in terror.)

MONA!?

(AMY pushes him away, and he sprawls helplessly. **AMY**
speaks into the phone.)

AMY. You should see his face.

(short pause)

Oh, I'll give him your love.

(short pause)

Get ready. You'll want to hear this.

(She lays down the phone.)

(She picks up the glass of poisoned wine, brings it to her lips, then lowers it.)

(She walks around **ADRIAN***, who writhes in pain.)*

AMY. *(continued)* Mona and I met in the hospital and became...how should I put this? Sisters under the skin. We discovered that the woman who turned me in was the woman you married. When Mona talked, you became all the men I'd ever hated.

(She brings the glass to her lips, then lowers it.)

Then I asked Mona what I could do for her. She said only one thing: she wanted to hear you die. Slowly and painfully. You were right. Sex is at the bottom of it. Only a woman who loved a man as much as Mona loved you could hate someone as much as she hates you now.

(She brings the glass of poisoned wine to her lips, waits, then pours the contents over him.)

ADRIAN. Stop it!

*(***AMY*** puts down the glass.)*

I'll give you anything you want!

AMY. Forget it! This is what we want.

(shouting)

Ready, Mona?

(She kneels and plunges the knife into him. He screams, but in her rage she drives the knife in again and again. Finally, when she is exhausted, she stops. He lies still. She puts the knife in her bag. Satisfied that he is dead, she picks up the phone.)

It's over.

(She puts away the phone in her bag. She surveys the scene with satisfaction, puts away the knife, picks up her bag, surveys once more, and turns to put on her shoes. Before she does, she smiles, walks to the bar, picks up the bottle of poisoned wine, and extends it toward **ADRIAN***.)*

AMY. *(continued)* It's over.

   (She drinks lustily.)

   (The lights go out at once.)

   (CURTAIN)

PROPERTIES

Wine bottles and glasses for the bar
Suitcase
Attaché case
Mail
Wastepaper basket
Japanese porcelain
Painting
Rug
Knife for the bar
Amy's handbag
Short club
Amy's knife
Amy's cell phone